'What is on the other side of base reality? Ana Tewson-Božić conveys the peculiarity and disarray of psychosis in a kind of distressed, demented prose which from time lets in shafts of reality—going round friends' houses, interacting with classmates in college, ending up in hospital. Anyone who's ever been through the looking glass will recognise her account. Anyone who hasn't—Wonderland awaits.'
—John O'Donoghue

Ana
Tewson-Božić

CRUMBS

myriad **m**∞

First published in 2020 by
Myriad Editions
www.myriadeditions.com

Myriad Editions
An imprint of New Internationalist Publications
The Old Music Hall, 106–108 Cowley Rd,
Oxford OX4 1JE

First printing
1 3 5 7 9 10 8 6 4 2

A CIP catalogue record for this book
is available from the British Library

ISBN (pbk): 978-1-912408-40-5
ISBN (ebk): 978-1-912408-41-2

Designed by WatchWord Editorial Services, London
Typeset in Dante by www.twenty-sixletters.com

Printed and bound in Great Britain
by CPI Group (UK) Ltd, Croydon CR0 4YY

For the burnt

To have faith is precisely to lose one's
mind so as to win God.
—Søren Kierkegaard

Tata

When my father was a young beatnik, he was visited by a light-engulfing orb of almost human proportions, small enough to make its way through the old, shuttered window of the shack in Croatia.

He took acid once, and then lost his speech for a month. He told me not to mess with that stuff.

Afterwards, the Serb would sit and smoke and watch the eye in the wood of the scabby door to the courtyard and it seemed to be the eye of Satan, or Sauron, overseeing all that we did there.

Some places hold the ancient power of a community. The neighbours chatter to me and my acid trip. I am transported higher. The door in the yard watches, as it watched my father, it guards the house I'm tripping in.

In this place, I see heaven. I am buoyed by the souls of the relatives in their homes around me, buoyed by the fact that they'd known and liked me. With these powers, I see fragile bodies rise through a church steeple and crumble into ash against the ceiling. I see great alien eyes and tongues of steely poison poised to greet us at our deaths. They see me back and I never felt so much terror.

Butch has seen it all before, he says on the walkie-talkie.

I wake when I've got too close to the reptilian all-seeing eyes. I go to the bathroom and splash water on my bovine face. I hold meat. I have breasts that are soft and pliable; Butch feels them and the acid tingles. The whole place becomes a sink-hole, a toilet bowl—we all spin down the drain with the sounds of plumbing an opera.

During my first psychotic episode, I was taken in by my parents. Tata was the devil, Mama an angel of light, a willow woman. I threw Faust at my father's feet in a holy rage. Woodward played *Dark Souls* on his Xbox and I saw the world in it. My mother was entangled in the roots of a tree, I saw her on the screen and rushed downstairs to find her sitting.

Mama and Tata

In a tall tower by the sea dwelt a woman of the waves. At the nape of her neck her hair did curl, though the rest of it she furiously tried to straighten. As she grew older, she sat glued to her laptop, a portal into other realms. Her hair losing pigment glowed brighter than it had in years. Her eyes glazed over like a wondering child's.

In these realms, her words flowed like pale fires and lapped at temples in a righteous rage, made quiet with only a secretary's tapping.

She'd been a typist for years, the keyboard was her piano, the trade she plied. She wiped words clean and examined them in wonder. But in the examination room, she ripped too heartily, and when away from the device, she would continue the excavation of language and thought, to the detriment of her tower-dwelling fellows.

Among these fellows was an old Eastern European gentleman—her lover. He had been scoured away almost completely, his ego a tiny shell he cultivated in secret. I was merely a lodger with them; I could not know fully the secrets they kept in their birdcage.

Their bedroom, you see, had been damaged by the son, in an argument with the woman. He'd punched holes in the door, as a teenager is wont to do, but the gentleman and the woman had not the funds to fix it. The war in Yugoslavia had rendered Yugotours obsolete, and the rise of booking holidays over the internet left a travel agent jobless—now delivering curries in a car bought with the woman's measly inheritance.

So, the woman, she'd put up chicken wire over the holes, cut into the doorframe to fix it. It was very pretty and French—or the perceived French of one who reads *House & Garden*—but it let loose the couple's every sigh, and the house and I, we heard them.

In the dead time before dawn, the gentleman woke up sick. He hobbled to the bathroom like a parody of the brave father I'd known, to vomit and heave. The woman could not believe him so grievously ill, but I knew it was slow death coming—the clouds were claiming his bones, sucked so dry in the flames. These are the secrets they've kept from me.

The secrets of the bowl (a poem)

Folk barely wash in this fell mansion, instead we
Breed bats, and at our desks have luncheon.
But the bowl knows more than any of we do,
The bowl has seen and eaten our sweaty loads
and gulped them down, down, down.
When the lid closes, the cats rush in and sit
On windowsills in pretty poses, this is just before
They maul a bird or some winged insect and
Play with its imminent corpse.
All breaks in the routine.
Everything's dirty and everything's clean.
I must bow down to the toilet:
God's greatest machine.

Catboy

Catboy is a Korean man. The moniker was bestowed
as a way to talk secretly about him to friends. He
had cats. Lots of cats. His milky torso was covered
in scratches—it was sexy, but we spoke not the same
tongue as tongues flashed in mouthy kisses to movies
with subtitles. After the affair ended, language being a
big part of both our inner worlds, unable to express pain
or pleasure except in sighs, I held a torch, I obsessed. In

my mind's psychic eye, he was there communicating through the ether: I saw his torso pumping, I saw his mouth smiling ghostly blue eyes. He was an anomaly. I was a schizophrenic. With too many analogues and an imagination vivid and romantic, I slid into visions.

I convinced myself my phone was racist, so threw it into a facility toilet, already partly blocked with car parts and banana skins. Catboy was not impressed with the homage. Alone in his flat sat he, a cat on each shoulder, like feathered accoutrements on an invisible blazer.

I, in hospital, started a war on the patients— I called them humanzees and myself Jesus. Without confidence I was weak, yet with too much I became a bully; Catboy had bullied me, too. When we had sex, his paws kneaded my rice stomach. I don't think he meant to ridicule, but it felt unclean.

A vagina is
A flower which opens up
Like an umbrella.

Butch and the teenaged years

There were ring-leaders in the group who were, in some part, responsible for the hideous outcomes of the members thereof. One of these 'commanders', as some were wont to term them, was a buxom lad who we'll call Butch. He had the ruddy glow of a Bull Terrier and was almost twice the bruiser of any bruiser I had laid eyes upon before.

The first time we met, I was at the home of a jolly neighbourhood lad ('heart of gold', they said of him) sitting safely upon a sofa, when descended the beast, eyes ablaze with an arm unfolding to curl around me.

As I was new to the bunch, and only a girl, brave fellows quickly stepped in to reprimand him and to forewarn me of the advances I was to receive. We smoked some more spliffs and he told me about how he wanted to abuse me in a bathtub. Later, these fantasies would come to pass with girls of a similar age, but without the necessary troops to rally and defend them. When he tried to train my addled cranium toward his crotch, the boys jumped up quickly.

I only laughed at his rabid face, and my mania— heightened by drugs and youth—served to satiate and appease the whims of chance, so that the demonic acts discussed and attempted would not then come to pass upon mine own head. I had swerved the fates so far in the story, at least, but woe be it to the girls whose fortunes I had tempted with childish laughter.

In later years, I would become as much a wretch as Butch, and we would meet in minds upon great cosmic highways, and we'd grind out our bodies just to sniff another mangy dog's tail.

Wargames

This lad, Butch, would take the boys on scavenging hunts around the fields when they'd all swallowed a mushroom or four, and dole out military responsibilities to each player—this made taking drugs a real adventure, real magic. The players, like me, simply laughed, and so fuelled the monster—who later would eject himself and be ejected from this society, a source of continued nightmares for the whole sorry team: candlelit and wined, we'd talk in hallowed giggles about his exploits, real and imagined, we'd talk about his stories.

This time, we were all sitting around the table when Butch sauntered in. He put his arm up on the wall and drawled, 'Well, well, well, children, what have we here?'

The place silenced; blankets of stoned holiness shut the lid on the jokes of before and all there was was Butch and his dog-leer.

'Sergeant Jones,' he woofed, staring at the boy, 'what is the protocol?'

The boy giggled and searched for an answer, 'Well, sir, it's like this, we were all watching the war play out here on the tablecloth, the Germans landed readily and stormed the base, man down, man down.'

Others began to make vague remarks, too, but without the fervour of Jones.

'HOW COULD YOU ALLOW SUCH INSO-LENCE?' Butch directed all his power at the forces, laying a hand of assurance upon the shoulder of the plucky Jones.

We scoffed, but were frightened. A sour mood swept over the place, a mood mingled with the adventure and wonder of the mushrooms, and many felt they had to leave the table for the garden, or some other likely spot, while Butch gathered his squadron. Jones laughed nervously under the great paw.

'Why do we need to fight a war all the time, Butch?' said I.

'Because it's a man's business, little girl. Be gone.'

And I sat on anyway and listened and scoffed again.

The war was incomprehensible, it chattered, and boys threw shapes of vigorous manhood around the little room, so that eventually I went and found

Woodward for a quiet chat and some smokes in the garden with the womenfolk, boys and girls both.

'This is *China*, boys. This is no play for layabouts, pansies, none of your dirty ilk.' Butch's refrain carried out like your father calling the cat. People huddled in the chill outside the gambling table, delirious to be away from the play of souls within.

Butch continued, 'In 'Nam, my friends, there are no winners or losers. Only losers.'

'And winners,' let in Jones, sneaky as a tart. 'And whores.'

They all liked this—we liked the joke outside too, but we didn't understand. We were staying away from the war against the outside; the great battle for dishonour conjuring within.

'We need a mission tonight, boys. Take position.'

And they shuffled to sort of stand up amidst beer cans and debris, and clink glasses in merriment. They went down the park.

Later, a religious boy called Ben picked crumbs of MDMA from floorboards and sucked them up his nose, but that is a few years later, and another soul.

The in-group has since disbanded, as the realisation of what we started those years ago crept in, we soldier-like found our pathways through the mire.

In houses such as this, the little bands of miscreants find their churches. These children found holiness in front of cigarettes, alcohol and drugs, as others find theirs in front of computers—networks of crazies, each pared down to the basic elements of humanity, freed of social structures, so as to appreciate a whole, to see the fragile conspiracies afoot more clearly.

When we reached adulthood, we were all— disorderly as we were—let into the secrets that the elders had kept from us, the secrets of the conspiracy of socio-political order. It had been brewing for some years, since Voyager left the Solar System, since the LSD trials, and the continued wars of man, and only a true addict could see it so clearly.

Julja

I am of a certain age—older than twenty-one—and so I suffer from necrosis, which I treat with E45 Cream.

In the facility, Cecilia cries, 'Fuck me, you whore!' and, 'I like a fat one—yesss…'

We say, 'Yessir, Please, sir, Thank you, sir,' on the Women's Ward. We bustle around the dispensary, and then we swallow it all, the garishly coloured nectars, and lick the rest from frothing lips.

'Beb,' she says, 'Hannah, beb, shut the fucking door.' She calls me Hannah—it is my English name. My Yugoslav name means July. I am the height of summer. Then she howls like that damn Wolfin does, 'Awooga!' Long and piercing like flutes, it cries the way my vision blurs when they come for me. Butch feels the ants sting as the wind reaches him there, too.

'Boys,' he talks into his hand, 'boys, can you hear me?'

Biz was on the boat and says, 'Captain?'

'This is the Captain,' says Jones. 'What can we do to help you today?'

I lie back, arms resting against my hair, belly out, do nothing.

'Oi, Woodward?' I muse.

'Yes, nurse?'

Nothing.

Jones

Jones had style. He worked in a used-clothing store and dressed like a toff or a sailor. A man of the woods, trapped in the cities that he loved. He was a functioning drug addict and held down degrees, honours, and a job paying one hundred and forty pounds a day.

He had a long-term girlfriend who he didn't know what to do with—she elfin, he a bard. His mind was woozy with thoughts of conquests never to be. What he'd do was, he'd charm a girl until she was ready and aching, then he'd saunter off into the night, or so he claimed.

Jones was enamoured with Butch, as were we all. The latter had a brutish charisma and acne vulgaris which had been cut into forming early wounds, making him all the fiercer in the ensuing battles. He was our very own Bukowski.

In front of women, Jones would call himself a feminist, but after a few beers and exposure to Butch's pheromones, that sentiment would pass like wind from the bowels.

Becoming alien

I'd found the key to my adulthood lying innocuously on the floor of a friend of the computer world, one of Woodward's people. I picked it up. It was a USB. His eyes instantly left the screen, pupils large from the influx of darkness in the room beyond the screen.

'Take it,' he said. 'But be careful, for you are of the outside.'

I plugged in the sleek device and up cropped pages upon pages of the tribe's exploits, being writ as I observed, being writ by the network of them all over the world. I typed back. Artists and song lyrics flickered across the screen as my words, in separate browsers, were auto-edited by the machines. I could not tear away my eyes, and felt my brain pounding with an excess of chemicals.

The computer flashed *LISTEN* and a music folder appeared.

I looked up at my friend for some sort of answer.

'Just take it home,' he said, 'and clear your mind. A user will input what you need.'

Schizophrenia and the Computer

The sun came through the sweaty window. I rested my head against the cold dew of the pane and finally turned off the computer.

The computer turned on again. Black lit the screen and a user started inputting: *Would you like to be prompted? I'll prompt you missus, oo-er, do you like it?*

My type responded in caps, so I must have been scared. *SAFE MODE*, I said.

14

The user logged off and the computer went back to sleep.

A few moments later, the computer fired to life again. Squirming bodies covered the screen as we, separate, made our connection. This first connect lasted for three days.

Mud, human forms, and a perpetual horniness permeated the experience, until I became dry as the bones that started to take the place of the screen bodies.

I imagined the user was Biz, the heart-throb of the group, the pusherman, with flowing black locks like a Davidoff commercial at night. Biz was into old cars. He wore a suit and all the girls had slept with him.

At some point the sleep deprivation and the journey into a world beyond my means, blew out my brains and I was taken. For the next few days, I became doomed to pick holy crumbs of wheat cakes from floorboards in penance for what I had experienced. Each of us had a different crumb to pick.

During this time, many items appeared as if from nowhere in the spare room I inhabited. Where once it was empty there came tokens. A brand-new

CD arrived, wrapped in plastic, with Butch's name scrawled across the top.

I put it into the computer and a new phenomenon occurred: I was issued with a mission—only this time it was not in the drunken jests of youth.

It started with a story:

The drugs were the pathway into the nether realms; we all were programmed as youths to initialise the transformation they set up for us.

I pressed a button to cease it—my brain being blown, I couldn't follow a narrative easily. This was a trait programmed into my generation.

An alien appeared on the screen, all in pink, with a halo of fluctuating pixels. I heard a voice in the room, evil and rasping say, 'We took you in your youth.'

A girl appeared on screen. It was the I of long ago, at some forsaken party with Butch and the others, only this time I had a halo and an alien beside me. I saw the kitchen and Butch's troops in crisp black and white. Their talk was repelling the pink fire that was engulfing me and the others. It was the kids in the garden they were after, especially Woodward, and I felt an overwhelming need to protect him.

The screen went white and a new message was given: *We have built a cure. The cure is the user system. You have been emptied. You are now being in-putted. Do not turn off your computer.*

A Big Pharm logo cropped up. For years the company had been administering drugs to the masses—we all knew, but had no inkling of what for.

I went to turn it off, the machine, and the room began to throb. My finger hovered over the power switch. A police siren sounded from the street and so I took the finger away. It was shaking.

The computer whirred and I took out the CD. I called up my friend.

'Hey.'

'Hey.'

'So we heard about what happened, the glitch. It's started, but you got given an 'in' into Butch's world, you don't want that.'

'What do I do?'

'You switch user, or you get taken. That's how it works until you've in-putted more. So far Butch has your sexuality, and you have his plans, but you didn't download them properly, we'll need to re-jig the config.'

A pulsing heart appeared on the screen and the words *it's going to be okay*. Then the entire room began to pulse again. On the phone, my friend said I must let it happen, that it was all part of an old hippie idea to save the future generations from the same curse, the experiments in bioengineering that had led us to this conundrum.

I let the computer change my surroundings. It took some of my visions and gave me a new lamp shade and a plate of meatballs.

'These will keep up your strength,' it told me.

As soon as I'd swallowed the gift, the doorbell rang.

A cyborg stood there with a parcel. It was a package to alleviate the symptoms of the past. Instructions within informed me that this was part of a worldwide test upon my generation, the generation that would safeguard the planet by separating from each other, by reconnecting through the robots and the others who had picked up the signals.

Jocelyn

Jocelyn loved sex and the stars. She controlled the weather. She lifted skinny fists into the ether and rain fell with her tears. She functioned as a psychotic. She called it being spiritual and consulted runestones for the smallest of the minutiae. Would she go out tonight? she asked.

I was not so lucky. I couldn't hold down a job with my extreme episodes. Once, I shat in the shower—I never told a soul. The full story is: the medication had me constipated and massaging my arse in the shower. A log or two fell out. I placed them in the bowl and cleaned up. It was a very degrading time.

Before the medication, I cried. I'd often turn up at Jocelyn's mansion in messy rags with a bloated face, and Jocelyn's dad would answer the door and joke, 'You look normal today.' I'd shrug off my poncho and walk up flights to the cloaked lamps in my friend's room, and we'd sit on the balcony smoking spliffs till the tears dried.

I used to watch videos of dolphins playing in marine parks just to feel the tears streak my cheeks, to wretch and sob at the injustices. When people around me died, I would self-medicate; in the dangerous planes between life and death I'd stumble concrete stairs and fall and puke blood into a gutter while Amy held back my hair and Woodward dialled an ambulance. The A&E staff at the weekends had little time for my kind and I'd awake groggy on a stretcher and stumble home calling Biz to meet me, but he'd never answer.

Sometimes Woodward and Jocelyn would wait outside for me and ferry me back as I cried.

Plato said tears were a release, but tears without emotion are just a bodily function—no better than a shit in the shower for comfort.

Julja

I sat with Jocelyn in the park. The adults automatically lowered their eyes when they saw us. I thought that they were privy to an old secret and she and I were being initiated into a new movement.

As we spoke, we felt for the first time a lack of ease in our conversation, for our animal energies had been converted into foods and gifts, and the style of communication we had always employed was rendering anew.

'I'm against the whole thing,' she said. 'It's a form of bullying, however magical it may seem.'

'But who are the bullies? I don't think it's really Butch doing this, I heard he disappeared. It's all designed by Big Pharm.'

'It's the very people who've disappeared that are fighting this thing,' she said. 'They input and output and just swap so that nothing is taken by the companies. I made a fire the other day and the computer showed me all these images of cheese. Now the idea of cheese sickens me.'

A youth walked by eating a Cheese String. We had conjured the scene somehow, we were part of the cycle.

'Maybe we can't make any fires, maybe we can't go outside now and that's the mission.' I think of Woodward's wide eyes at his screen, and his friend with the USB.

'Screw the mission. That was child's talk.'

'I don't think it can be stopped once they've exploded your head. We drank the offerings in those days, we didn't know, and now we have nothing. We have to go through this and try to meddle as little as possible. We become users or we become aliens, those are the choices.'

She handed me a small green pill and said, 'Not so.'

I looked at it.

'I picked these up in South America,' she said. 'Over there they have a system to restore the brain's chemistry so that you can switch user groups, you don't have to stick with Butch, and Biz, and the others.'

'But the user system is out of my control. I connect with whoever my subconscious demands. These pills will widen it, they might make me an alien.'

'There are no aliens, only different user groups. It's other people connecting. The aliens are just a collective image we've all created through the system. The aliens are the robots, or our ideas of otherness.'

'I don't understand.'

'Nobody understands, we just start to adjust.'

We sat and watched as the people wandered past and went home to play. I took the pill and my head began to throb. She took me to her place to lie down.

Jocelyn's house was stately, and her pills were pure. We were of different classes and her gift, like the gift from the computer world, did not agree with my physiology. I had been created to be expendable, to be religious.

She turned on her computer.

Two women filled the screen. They were 3-D images of ourselves. We'd both created them. They were the present. I imagined myself bigger and the image zoomed.

The doorbell rang and I heard Jocelyn usher me in and then there I was in the room while I lay on the sofa dreaming.

I went over to myself and sat close to my legs. I could feel the pressure of my body beside me and looked into my own eyes. Our pupils widened and widened until all was black and I was gone.

When I awoke, I was no longer on Earth. I had been initiated. I thought I must have failed my mission completely.

Space

The room on the spaceship was circular. Black beams cradled a roof to the stars, and white panels filled the wall space. The bed was central, and I was prostrate upon it.

I heard the sounds of people in a room beyond. They were laughing. I felt nothing.

I stood up to follow the voices.

Barely aware of my body, I fumbled with switches until the glass door to the corridor swept open. A white tube led in a curve towards the next room, the room from whence the voices seemed to emanate.

I wandered to the left and stopped to listen at the metal door. Everything was muffled, but I could make out accents and tones that were undeniably Earthly. My hands were sweaty. I could feel their moisture, but my body was no longer my own. I had grey talons in the place of my human pinions.

This realisation overwhelmed me and I was afraid to speak, though I felt I must try to contact the humans beyond the door.

I knocked.

'Hello?'

The voice was deeper than mine own, but it carried the standard British accent I had acquired as a child. This appeased the instincts not yet lost to me. My humanity remained.

All sound from within ceased for a moment and then I heard the anxious tones of a party deciding a course of action. One voice carried a calm with it and moved closer. The door creaked open.

Among the granite figures, taloned like me, and warty, a laboratory was laid out. Great flasks bubbled noxious fumes and we all breathed deeply. I felt an ancient knowledge seep into me. We were the forefathers, taking the places of the forefathers before us, concocting experiments to exact upon the next generation of humans.

Below us stretched a vast Earth, where our bodies, disconnected from our minds, continued, run on the instincts we had in-putted to the computers.

Each of the party also had a screen before them. Upon the screens were maps, with cross-hairs that the aliens used to recycle emotions between the Earthlings. Most often they would guide them towards different foods and chemicals. They used a touchpad.

I lay out on the sofa for weeks before I returned. They fed me intravenously as my eyes flickered and tokens built up in the room. All the lost books of strangers gathered there: an antique *Gardener's World* digest, a collection of Baudelaire's poetry, a magazine about porcelain dolls.

People would come to pay respects to one who had not returned.

On the spaceship, I played with the people I had met in the debauchery of youth. I'd give some of them job offers, desperately trying to hold on to any love I'd felt for them, as daily I turned further into stone.

The stone we were made from was created in the ship. It reacted with Earthly matter, though it was alien itself. In this form I could make creations for those with the requisite technology in their machines.

I became obsessed with Woodward.

He had been a quiet boy of average height with a shock of blonde curls. In front of my cross-hair he appeared as an angel. I saw him sit beside my sickbed and hold my hand and chant. Jocelyn's computer fed us the room's data each time she switched on.

In Jocelyn's house there lived three generations, all following different protocols, informed by different user groups.

Her father answered his phone. It was an old model that linked into a building in Russia. It gave him the voices of his card-playing troupe. Their job was to play weekly games, with the suits corresponding to the members of their family. The old men were represented by the kings, their wives the queens, and their offspring were jacks, and all below.

As they win and lose, so their families are affected.

I stole the cards one day.

Up in the spaceship, I built a huge house from them to represent Jocelyn's. At that time, my own room had been at a hostel and did not hold the same powers as that of the family home I would end up in—I found out that this was one of the reasons I had been taken.

Each card is stacked so that it is partitioning and partitioned from another. Together the cards so balanced, provide supports for the house. If they topple, so the worldly house topples with them. Of course, the cards eventually fall and some are lost between the fingers of the mind and the deck becomes short a few. As the men play their game, they must search for the missing cards between boxes and floorboards, all eating away at their time. One kind soul retrieves a joker, an ace, or even an unassuming two; the cards are shuffled and their game begins anew.

One of the men now employs trickery to win his battle—a shark's move more deadly than teeth—he uses sarcasm to bring shakes to the other players. Their brewing epilepsy is a side-effect of this tribal system. They shake for the lives of their offspring, but some of us are beyond their means. Some of us still dwell outside.

Ben the Jew

We return to Ben the Jew, as Big Dave coined him, picking drugged crumbs from floorboards, way up in some spaceship of his own. When he returned to his body, all the gifts that had sprung during the heady days of his awakening mocked him. Who was he to read of Baudelaire when his meatballs had not been served? For upon his return from the laboratory, there were no more offerings for him from the gods.

He searched for further clues, as I would come to do, in back alleys and shop fronts alike, but there were none. We were experiments only, with no great truth to be found at the end. Instead the alien truth would be discovered in the centre of things, and adult life would consist of unravelling and forgetting in order to survive.

It has been some time since the zealous ascent, and even longer since the army games of youth. In ageing, I hark back to the stacks of cards, on my way to join an old man's playing circle. The ascent has caused my human brain to become misdirected. This is called 'thought disorder' and Big Pharm has its claws deep into that. Once we aliens have ascended, been chewed and spat back again, it becomes harder to function as a human being. We realise that in fact the majority aren't privy to the secrets of experience-swapping and the user system. They have simply acted as harbingers in our misdirected ascensions.

Those at their computers input their functions subconsciously and the aliens regurgitate them in a manner we can never really comprehend. We pare ourselves down to the most basic grains of reality. This is where the crumbs play their part as the wafers of the great religion of psychotics. Big Pharm provides the drugs to secure us back into reality. Synthesised crumbs take the place of those crumbs of hash that used to fill my tobacco pouches.

Butch had been training his mind for subterfuge for years, and passed this training on to the wayward youths whose imaginations he could twist.

His realm was the wargames.

Ben represented Judaism, purely because of his moniker.

I'd begun cultivating the cults.

These frameworks were the basis for psychosis.

29

My initial thought was that a magician had hypnotised me for a secret-camera show. It was the most logical explanation, but upon searching for cameras and finding none I became obsessed with ideas of conspiracy and a New World Order of old men who'd been to Eton and were controlling us through placing chemicals in our water systems. I worried that witches were conducting rituals affecting my mind. I thought Woodward would die because I was making him channel the souls of those I missed from Korea.

Never once did I assign reverse culture shock, stress and psychosis to my experiences, I just followed the narrative as it meandered, and deluded myself into deeper and deeper shit.

Sixth Form

It became clear one night, playing telltales with Catboy in Korea, that it was a small player in Butch's fantasies who held my heart, one so special his name had become hallowed. He became a ghost. A ghost can be a very dangerous thing. You can tell yourself it's not real and you're in no danger, but it presses on to your legs making them weak, making your mind wander.

Back in the school days, Butch and the gang had a film studies class together (all being of a middle-class catchment, more or less, and so given such choices as film and media, pottery, and photography to make their studies of).

I fell in love with Biz in that way—I think it was purely based on seating arrangements—he was glowering directly in front of me, covered in make-up. Catboy was hidden, back always to me, a small player in the game, just about able to turn a sharp nose about to argue some point with me before being nothing but skinny back and shoulders.

Wait, no. Catboy was not there. He was in Korea, glowering in his own classroom. Only I mix up Biz and Catboy as I love them so. I think, if only Catboy would call and Biz would give me his hand.

The neighbourhood lad, who loved crisps, Walkers, Monster Munch, all of them, sometimes sat near me, so we bonded. But mostly, I bonded with a slutty girl called Nazilla, she was just open, really, and boobs large for her age. We were all of an age where sex was legal and executed, though I had abstained—not for lack of wanting, but for having come to this school from a girls' grammar. I didn't understand my power yet.

Abductee

I woke up standing in the middle of the park clutching a Jack of Hearts with an eye scrawled on it in marker. I was looking at the stars and spinning.

Around in the blackness I heard the whispers of those who had witnessed me—some were gathering for a ritual in the nearby graveyard, the witches. I could see their fire licking, and shadowy figures around the light—they were waiting for me, my mission had started. They waited for me to join Biz's coven, to choose him.

I stumbled out of the field and on to a street and sat in someone's front garden weeping into human hands. A young woman with dark hair walked by, she was confiding in a friend about her relation to my exploits. She knew Biz, she had been with Biz, and they remained friends; she saw me and giggled into a cupped hand as they passed. They knew about the tests.

Butch had walked this route before me, had traversed every alleyway of the cosmic empire, but I was lost, swimming in my head.

A woman who was against the-sort-of-thing going on at the graveyard—the-sort-of-thing I was hopelessly aware was in honour of my recent descent—took me by the shoulders and asked me if I was okay.

'Something terrible is going to happen.'

'Oh dear.' She cradled me. 'It's okay.'

'I just want to go home.'

And with an arm about me she led me all the way to my parents' house, where I produced a key and went inside.

I found my mother sitting in the darkness at her computer, ferreted away in the furthest corner of the house.

We had a row and her face became changed into that of an old wizard I had met at the pub and had shown some of my writings to. He liked them and, upon hearing of my interior landscapes, had gained a power over my world. He, my mother, grinned at my discomfit.

I cried, 'Get out of my house!'

'This is my house,' she responded, angered. 'You get out.'

And I began to go. It was then she softened and in her face I saw Biz say, 'I love you. You can stay.' Her hair shone in the lamplight.

Sated I went up to the cubby hole that constituted my temporary abode. I tried to get some sleep, but giddy with love I recalled 'the test' and my communication with them.

The test

The test was being carried out by a secret society upon myself and my comrades. It was a test of intelligence, endurance and love. I had once loved Ben, but now loved Biz, and Woodward loved me, while Amy was in love with Woodward, and Jocelyn Butch; Woodward's computer friend loved Jocelyn, and his love endured the years. Woodward's love for me was the purest I had, and he, witnessing, perhaps instigating the tests, had awaited me in his room. He saw me ascending to the spaceship and watching him, he saw it on his screen. When he realised I was in love with Biz and he was merely an icon, something to protect, he gave up his clutches on reality and turned to gold.

He had stood in his room, up out of the chair away from his computer and really listened to the flood of voices. They told him to die, to become perfectly still, to not breathe. They told him that if I were true, I would come to him. At that moment, the whole tribe was relayed the same message. A few of us lay on the floor and attempted it, to stay dead still, but only Woodward, heart of gold, succeeded. I remember being flooded with sound: 'NOW, NOW,' they said. And I dropped to the floor like a stone and held my breath, but as I turned the colours of death I exhaled, and then inhaled the carpet and lived. Woodward stayed statue still.

The aliens crafted a real statue of him to replace the fallen soldier and took him up with them.

I had killed him. I wept.

Biz was waiting for me, he had won the game of intellect, I knew this for I knew he could complete a cryptic crossword without assistance, and I wasn't far behind. It was little clues like this that had me convinced of the aforementioned webs. I grabbed my iPod to send a message to Biz, for I couldn't let him die like Woodward, waiting for one who had failed to be brave enough to confront the witches at the graveyard and join his society.

Biz commanded the ghouls, the shadowy figures I'd seen whispering. He didn't flinch when the voices told us to be still, he knew it was trickery, but how I loved him and how I worried.

I played a song for him, in his home, waiting. I knew he was there, for his music choices appeared on my tiny screen, they were love songs to me, exhausted, they were gothic lullabies and soothed me. I sat in bed and put on Kate Bush's 'Running Up That Hill'. I must've drifted off for a moment. I awoke to a voice telling me to go to him, to run up the hill, to follow Kate's madness and win worldly acclaim. It was 3am. I had to tell him what we'd done to Woodward.

I looked raggedy in a long, holey cardigan, a nightie over jeans and some old boots—Biz was always immaculate, but I needed him to see me desperate, to see my love, so I ran. I did not run without aid, I had my headphones in my ears like stoppers, and they directed me, left, right, straight to a house not far from my parents'. I had a pink penknife with an inlay of a pin-up girl for protection.

I went down some steps to the door of the house I'd been directed to, and armed and ready, knocked a few times. I was sure he waited within.

A female voice, unfamiliar, 'Who's there?'

I gave my full name: Julja B_____, and asked for Biz.

'I don't know what you're talking about. Go away!'

I stood for a moment.

'Go away!'

I left.

Ben had been tested for true love before and found her—he was once my love and could help me through the tribulations I faced. He lived with Amy, his lady, Esme, and our computer friend—they would know what to do. Hungry but unaware of it, filled with adrenaline and dopamine flooding my brain, I stumbled to their house a mile away. It was on the way to Biz's mum's house where I knew I had to go. I would, however, have to pass Woodward's house to get there. What if his mum came out to get me, what if she knew it was my fault?

They were having a party when I got there— Ben did not seem pleased to see me but allowed me inside. The computer friend gave me some beer. Jones was there and was making thrusting gestures with his crotch, which I found highly disturbing. I asked if Woodward was okay.

'I'm sure he's fine,' said the computer friend.

The party was ending and Jones suggested I get some rest in the spare room on a sofa bed, he would be staying on a mattress nearby. He was stoned and tired. I couldn't sleep and Jones disgusted me, so I went into the now empty living room/kitchen area and turned on the radio and a laptop. The radio played a babble of worries and I wrote a love letter to Biz on the laptop, sure that he was still waiting for me, and sure that Butch, my compatriot, would relay my messages. Sure enough, I received answers on the screen.

Biz was being really romantic and suggested I write our story in all its epic glory. I couldn't even begin to do it at the time, or for many years after, as I came to realise it was only my story and my delusion. This here that you read is an account of how I came to the realisation, prompted by Big Pharm and professionals, that I must discount my experience and train myself to base reality only.

One firmly rooted in reality was Ben's girlfriend, who at this time was waking up for work. She came in, asked if I was okay and began making a coffee. I said that I was and went to sit in the cold, dawning garden. She dallied over me a little, but loath to be late for work, she disappeared. I psyched myself up for the journey to Biz's house.

The computer friend has a name but I dare not pen it. He is a metalhead and wears a vintage leather biker jacket. I asked him if I could procure it for my walk, he, half awake, agreed to it. I put it on and felt braver. I had one thing left to do before I could go to my destination and that was to talk to Ben, who lay upstairs somewhere. I rudely poked my head into Amy's room on the way, but she was sleeping. A door ahead lay open and I went in. Ben, ginger afro swaying, swung around scared.

'What. The. Fuck,' he said.

'I need to talk.'

'It's 7am, what are you doing here?' And then he got really angry and shouted, '*Fuck off!*' with tears of rage and confusion in his icy eyes.

I stumbled out of the house crying and ran till I was at the school field and out of breath.

My phone rang.

The job

A few weeks before, I had been staying in the hostel with a band of miscreants. I had washed in a bucket and put on smart clothes and even heels and gone to a week of unpaid training to work at a private English school. I didn't believe in the values of such an institute, making over-worked kids pay high fees for underqualified teachers to riddle them with extracurricular homework. The man who ran the place was a sleaze and really liked my little heels.

I got the job. I hadn't eaten all week so I could pay for the trains to Richmond, where the wealthy abide. The call was about the job.

'Is this Julja B_____?'

'Yes.'

'You were scheduled to teach a class today, but you haven't turned up.'

'I'm sorry, something terrible's happened and I can't work for you.'

'Well—'

I hung up. I had somewhere to be.

I tottered to my feet and trudged the rest of the way to Biz's mum's house where she answered the door, surprised. I was led up to Biz's room where he sat at his computer. He was even less pleased to see me than Ben.

Your mama and mine

Mate, your mum eats hay right off the bale and then feeds it to cows, mate, then she picks up lovely white stones, but it's just dried dog poo.

A waking dream

Silent Hornets reigned.
They reclined, hidden upon the
Lawns and sat atop the clear,
Cold waters.
The girl was calling to me.
But only in their midst did
I understand the nature of her
Cries.
They settled between my
Breasts and laid
Hideous mounds across my body.
I ran sluggishly through
The still river.
Shivered but didn't notice.

Biz

Biz had been sitting at his computer all morning, watching my songs flash up, worrying. When I encumbered myself into his room, he was shocked, and his greeting was not a warm one. But I cried and he held me and I sputtered, 'You made me feel special.'

'You are special,' he said, letting me go. 'But I have to get to work and you have to go.'

I said, on my way out, a line I thought was pretty aware for my state of being at that time—perhaps my love made me lucid for a moment—I said, 'Well, winter is a good time for an existential crisis.'

When I left, I cried and ran like a hound to the nearest patch of grass, it was a cold and sunny day and the world had bitterly crisp edges.

Institutions

Home was the hospital where they fed us more and more pills and the incontinence pads piled up in the bathrooms. I began pissing in the garden. The other patients watched incredulously as, after dousing the plants newly potted, I performed a ritual dance upon the grass. The dance, as with my other seemingly incongruent pursuits, was paramount. It was a dance that spoke to aliens, to the voices of the dead I'd hear speaking to me from the moon; the dance kept the world spinning.

A psychotic sees the whims of the universe as directly connected to the pursuits of men. Individuals become symbolic of planets, and as we dance around each other, so the planets circulate.

In the canteen, I meet a real paedophile, and

we become friends. He is in his eighties, big-nosed with flushed flesh, and speaks with the dialect of the public schooled. He is a moon-like figure, he moons about a lost love when he was young, and hawks me, for my age reminds him of this would-be bride.

I am advised against this friendship.

The troll

What I'll do is, I'll tell a truth but deliver it in such an obnoxious way as to void all honesty about the Thing. Stripped will be its true meaning and cheapened and distant will it be shared, so anything I learned or felt about it really, cannot be focussed upon.

I am the worst sort of liar you'll ever meet, for oft are the most seemingly honest and open, the most sinfully unforthcoming. It is a showman's show of truth I deliver.

Oh, the ways I have done injustice to my perceptions when conveying them to others, for it is so terrifying to open up—that as the words float out, honest to a fault—so my soul and fresh emotions shrink away and those listening become objects of fear and paranoia, and in some way I am mocking them as I play with their attention, as though they were gormless puppets. Oh, I am loathsomely lonesome.

The gods

I finished masturbating in Heaven to the sounds of dogs barking. That was the last time I would feel pleasure in my body for years. Shortly after my stay in the house of the gods, I would be prescribed Risperidone, a strong chemical that spawned rashes, hair loss and dumbness.

I knew I was in Heaven when I saw the ladder and fresh paint. We were getting a make-over in the tower, we were so lucky. In a drawer, I found coloured candles shining with religion. They said *Happy Birthday*. I was being born unto the realm of gods: my father was Zeus, my mother Hera, my brother Apollo, and I was one year old, new, and anything could happen on this birthday. Or they were old candles from my niece's first birthday, nothing to do with me. Only everything had to do with me now I had found the centre of all the clues and conspiracies, and at the centre lay the Minotaur, the demon I'd let in.

There were focus groups and committees in the higher tiers of Heaven and they hand-picked my gifts; they consulted with Woodward and the others upon my tastes. I could hear them confer, all voices but Woodward's were faint, he was imploring they accept me despite the evil I carried with me.

I felt a sense of self-importance and, revelling in the moment, I cut off my hair and donned a black and white party dress. I looked like the girl in *Breathless*, and my brother caught my homage and noted it on the way up to play *Dark Souls*. The house breathed incest and when I hugged my father in thanks for allowing me there, I felt an erection and recoiled.

The horrors began. I ran from him to the bathroom and looked in the mirror where I saw myself sprout a moustache and become a man. I went to my room and put 'Gigolo Aunt' by Syd Barrett on. That would be my role in the realm, the gigolo. I was resigned to it and began to adorn myself accordingly.

In Chinese trousers and a blue waistcoat, open and bare underneath, I went to step out to the snowy streets below. My parents wrestled me and my flapping breasts from the doorstep.

Egomania

Outside, cars waited to help me escape from my parents' house, as they would wait in the hospital car park during my subsequent manias. I was all over the television and people were flooding to help me, they pitied me for losing Woodward in the mess. I packed a suitcase and brought it downstairs. My father tried to feed me, but the food contained human souls and I could not bear to consume it. It was punishment for sending Woodward to the other realm.

Dinner-table talk took on great import—there were scandals in the news, they were about me. I was, flooded with dopamine, the crux of all that occurred around me. I stepped into the yard and drew a face in the snow atop a recycling box as a message for the aliens.

On the boiler, lights blinked, another signal for me. I decided, staring at the LEDs, that I was not significant enough for the government to spike the water, but instead a jilted boyfriend had decided to put acid into the water to punish me and my family.

I went to the phone and called somebody at the hovel. I threw accusations at him, 'HOW COULD YOU DO THIS TO MY FAMILY?' He became agitated, and I began to cry, I threatened to call the police, but I never did—one never resorted to calling the pigs in my society.

Amy

Amy is strong, I wonder whether she is my friend or my carer. She comes to visit me while I'm incarcerated, my alien-given powers have no effect on her, she is solid.

When she leaves, I return to those who have passed. My family become conduits for those I have left behind around the world I had been travelling. Little gestures from my brother remind me so strongly of Woodward that he begins to speak to me through him. The longer we converse, and as hours turn small, my brother begins to sink into his pillows more and more until he becomes so small and fatigued by the mad connection that he sends me back to my room, the airing cupboard. I speak to many friends and lovers through my brother, I wonder that he hasn't berated me for my misuse of his mellifluousness.

Amy bullies into my delusions and has me watch an old Eurovision contestant on the computer. She says, 'I like her skirt,' and I come back to reality a little. We all share cigarettes.

I decide, while playing *Mario Kart* (not to win, but to amuse myself driving in circles, spitting up dust), that we are all part of a character's team. We three—my brother, Amy and I—are part of 'Team Toad', the smallest and fastest character. This team stands, ironically, for humility, and I swear my allegiance to it and all the members that I am, with great humility, assigning to it. It comprises friends who wear hoodies, friends who slouch, stutter, doubt, and in this way, with Amy looking at me sceptically, I begin to recover.

During my first 'recovery', I missed the immediacy and meaning I'd derived from my insanity, but once I'd been institutionalised as mentally unwell, I gladly accepted my re-emergence into civilised manners, though this admittance into a mainstream way of thinking carried with it a sense of shame about my previous behaviours. I couldn't have remained that way, though I had been free; I couldn't remain a woman constantly stripping bare of clothing, fully sexed, fully animal, it was an embarrassment. How could I marry the one self to the other? The disinhibited freedom seeker, rejector of societal convention, to the shy repenter, the taker of Risperidone.

Meanwhile, Butch.

Butch didn't need to drink that penitent Kool-Aid.
Butch answered to no substance. Butch teemed with
violence and hormonal highs unseen and untaken,
they surged within, and without was war and his
disposition was welcome.

His Afghanistan was full of Commies and Japs
and the notorious villains he worshipped, all swirling
in multicoloured atmospheres, blurred lines and the
sensations he experienced upon his skin.

Butch had died in the army, everybody knew.
A big military grade Jeep stalled in mud and the
spinning tyre triggered it, his head split in two.

Somehow Butch managed to survive, we cannot
ask how, but head reeling and spitting blunt goo, he
staggered to a rival bunker to bandage himself back
together. Just then, he heard an ominous rumbling
from above: an enemy plane, it was. Lights winked
at his one eye. His other cried a single tear.

The Ities moved fast in 'Nam and Butch moved
faster, quickly he bustled into a termite mound
situated politely behind the bunker and waited. Ants
nibbled his billowing face, but Butch was a hard-nut
and verily he allowed it.

I am the Wolfin

By the light of a gibbous moon only
Does the Wolfin ascend from the gloomy sea to visit
The growing of a smile,
And he smiles and bays, howling
Tunes to Venus, singing:
Awooga, Awooga!
And a tear rolls down smiling
Wolfin's cheek, and his gibbous head tilts
To one side, and he catches the eye.
He really does.
Oh, noble Wolfin, were there but a
Wolfina to company you on your way.

fin

Acknowledgements

To all at Myriad and New Writing South, I thank you, you kindly benefactors. I also must acknowledge Creative Future and Matt Freidson, who informed me I'd been selected for this opportunity on April Fool's Day, which I appreciate. And, especially, I would like to acknowledge Claudia Gould, who has a most charming email handle and suffered some bad luck with her foot during the initial stages of the mentoring process, having no effect at all on her deft editing abilities and enthusiasm for the work. Also, writing of editing abilities, to VHS—you know who you are.

About the author

Ana Tewson-Božić grew up in Belgrade and Berlin before moving to London and then to Brighton as a teenager. She has taught in South Korea, and has also worked as a refuse collector, care worker, cleaner and proofreader. She has spent significant time in mental institutions and is diagnosed with schizo-affective disorder.

About Spotlight

Spotlight Books is a collaboration between Myriad Editions, Creative Future and New Writing South to discover, guide and support writers whose voices are under-represented.

Our aim is to spotlight new talent that otherwise would not be recognised, and to help writers who face barriers, or lack opportunities, to develop their creative and professional skills in order to create a lasting legacy of work.

Each of our three organisations is dedicated to specific aspects of writer development. Together we are able to offer a clear ladder of support, from mentorship through to development editing and promotional opportunities.

Spotlight books are not only treasures in themselves but also beacons to other under-represented writers. For further information, please visit: www.creativefuture.org.uk

Spotlight is supported by Arts Council England.

'These works are both nourishing and inspiring, and a gift to any reader.'—Kerry Hudson

Spotlight stories

Georgina Aboud
Cora Vincent

Tara Gould
The Haunting of Strawberry Water

Ana Tewson-Božić
Crumbs

Spotlight poetry

Jacqueline Haskell
Stroking Cerberus: Poems from the Afterlife

Elizabeth Ridout
Summon

Sarah Windebank
Memories of a Swedish Grandmother